Clint Faraday
book forty two
A Smidgen of Murder

"A generous dollop of fresh creamery butter, a *touch* of mild curry, a teaspoon of nice fresh basil from my own garden, a *lit*tle salt, a dash of black pepper, and a *taste* of culantro!

"Bake for thirty five minutes at three seventy five. Chill, and add a *smidgen* of murder! Serve over curried chilled cheese pasta.

"Are you going away, with no word of farewell?

"Time to get dressed! I *do* want to look good for this!"

Contents

About the author

CD Moulton has traveled extensively over much of the world both in the music business, where he was a rock guitarist, songwriter and arranger and in an import/export business. He has been everything from a bar owner to auto salvage (junkyard) manager, longshoreman to high steel worker, orchid grower to landscaper, tropical fish farmer to commercial fisherman. He started writing books in 1983 and has published more than 350 books as of January 1, 2023. His most popular books to date are about research with orchids, though much of his science fiction and fantasy work has proven popular. He wrote the CD Grimes, PI series, and the Det. Nick Storie series, Clint Faraday series, and many other works.

He now resides in Gualaca, Chiriqui, Panamá, where he writes books, plays music with friends, does research with orchids and medicinal plants. He has lately become involved in fighting for the rights of the indigenous people, who are among his closest friends, and in fighting the extreme corruption in the courts and police in Panamá.

He offers the free e-book, *Fading Paradise*, that explains what he has been through because of the corruption.

CD is the discoverer of the Chadam Protocol for curing cancer.

Facebook page Ambrosia peruviana for cancer.

<u>*A Unique Recipe*</u>

"A generous dollop of fresh creamery butter, a *touch* of mild curry, a teaspoon of nice fresh basil from my own garden, a *lit*tle salt, a dash of black pepper, and a *taste* of culantro!

"Bake for thirty five minutes at three seventy five. Chill, and add a *smidgen* of murder! Serve over curried chilled cheese pasta.

"Are you going away with no word of farewell?

"Time to get dressed! I *do* want to look good for this!"

<u>*A Dinner Party*</u>
Clint read the notice for
The Oddball Gringo Gourmet Dinner Club
<u>Saturday nite, July 28, 6:30 PM</u>
you are invited as a member's guest to a
<u>(member: *Ben Longstreet*)</u>
<u>Dinner Party</u>
of the
Oddball Gringo Gourmet Dinner Club
at
Charles' Place

This meeting, each member will prepare a full favorite dinner for one. The dinners will then be placed on the tables at random. A number will be selected before seating and the diner will sit at that number. If you select your own plate, you will exchange the number.

Plates for any guests will be supplied by the member who invited that guest.

Member number:_010__
Guest(s) number: <u>17 & 18</u>

This notice will serve as your reservation.

"Hon, we're invited to a gourmet dinner. Want to go?" Clint Faraday, retired PI from Florida, asked of his wife, Tyna.

"Who invited us?" Tyna answered.

"Ben."

"Well, he's most certainly a gourmet's chef. Earl is even better. When is it?"

"Saturday."

"We can't, Clint. We promised to be at Mom's, remember? It's her birthday."

"Oh, yeah. I'll explain. It's a good excuse not to have to dress up. I don't do that bit anymore. Besides, we get to eat Ben and Earl's food all the time!"

They teased a bit. Nito, their four and a half year old son, came in to say he wanted to get the hell away from Bocas. He didn't like half the people there. They were a bunch of phony-asses!

"What now?" Tyna asked, coming out on the deck with Nicole, their two year old daughter.

"Oh, nothing. I was at The Grill with Samuél and some stupid gringas were there and they asked where our mothers were. I said I supposed you were here at home. One of them said it was outrageous that you'd allow a child to roam on the streets! Anything could happen!

"Samuél told her we aren't in Los Estados now and that nothing was going to happen all that awful.

"She said how old was he and he said five and

I'm four and a half. She started yelling about perverts and little boys and all that. I told her I didn't like that sex stuff. I would have to be older to even know what she was talking about.

"Stupid! She was going to call the police on you. Sergio was just outside so I called him. She said you were an unfit mother or something. then he said you were an excellent mother. She was ranting on like a silly fool. She said there were perverts all over the place and you were leaving me on the streets to be targets for them.

"I said if anyone tried anything with me I would yell and Sergio would shoot them. It was a little funny then. Sergio had to tell her that you can do anything you want if you're more than twelve or fourteen, but he definitely would shoot anyone who assaulted any child. Then she was yelling about police brutality when a cop would just shoot someone.

"I said perverts were horrible people who had to be stopped and I was in danger from them, but it was horrible if the police stopped them. She was stupid. She had to make up her mind.

"Then she said it was a parent's responsibility to raise a child with the knowledge there were people like that around. Sergio said it was pretty obvious that I knew more about that kind of thing than she did. It was as obvious that you were raising me right.

"She said you were putting me in danger. He said there wasn't any danger because I knew what to do. Yell. He would then shoot the pervert. The perverts who came here knew that was the law. No one would bother me.

"She said someone could grab me and cover my mouth to where I couldn't yell. He said, 'In a public park with two hundred people watching? Really? Maybe you could tell me how? No one would see?'

"She said people wouldn't want to be involved. He said this isn't the US. Anyone here would be involved if it was a child.

"She didn't say anything. One of the others said she thought she heard him say twelve or fourteen? I would still be a child!

"I said I'd be a child with experience and would know if I liked it or not. He would arrest them if I didn't like it. If I did, I wouldn't be yelling, would I?

"I left. All of them were yelling at each other. Samuél was laughing so much he couldn't even walk straight.

"I like the comarca. We don't have those silly nutcase biddies there."

"It's a different culture they know," Clint said. "It is a problem in the states and most cities. It's a problem in Panamá City. It's because there are too many people and they're raised with what we think of as weird ideas. The parents and the churches and the TV and the movies teach the wrong things to people when they're your age. I was scared to death to be left alone at night in Tampa. Tampa wasn't nearly as bad as some of those places.

"I had guys want to do things when I was fourteen or fifteen. I was terrified, even though they only asked me if I wanted to try it. I never did – at that age – and would probably have been as screwed up as they think you'll be if anything had happened. I would probably feel guilty and evil because I hadn't died fighting them."

"If you had to fight some big guy and he raped you, why would you feel guilty? *You* didn't do anything, *he* did!"

"That's the stupidity of teaching kids the wrong thing."

"If somebody raped me I wouldn't feel guilty. I would at least know if I liked it."

"If you liked it in that culture, you'd know you were already damned to hell," Tyna said. "I'll tell Ben we can't go."

"I don't believe in hell."

"That's not the point," Clint said.

"I know it."

Clint gave him the finger. He laughed. "See? I don't know if I'd like it, yet!"

Clint laughed. He thought about having that kind of conversation with a four and a half year old son in the states. It would never happen. Nito knew the finger meant, "Up your ass!"

They played and teased. Clint could picture the next time he talked with Sergio. He could guess what the conversation would be about. Sergio liked to bait that type of women with his "What's the big deal? You don't like sex? Bocas is a party town. Half the people who come here come for sex!" act.

Before they went to bed Clint said he had to agree with Nito. He'd much rather be living on the comarca. Maybe they could go on Monday. Five weeks in Bocas Town this time. The time before it was two months. The time before that was three months. This was a great place to visit for a week or two, but living here was getting to be a drag.

In the morning the family went fishing and boating with Judi Lum, Clint's attractive Oriental next door neighbor who helped him in a lot of his cases, her present boyfriend, John Marshall, and Ben and Earl, a gay couple who were also close friends who lived a short distance toward Bocas Town. They went to the smaller islands to the east for a picnic lunch and lazing around. Nito and

Nicole explored the island and brought Clint a strange orchid they found that was on a dead branch that had fallen, It would have died if left there.

They were chatting about whatever came up. Tyna told Ben that they couldn't go to the dinner because of her mother's birthday. Judi and John were going.

"It'll be fun. Those meetings usually are. We're a weird bunch!" Earl said. "We have some people who are just plain crazy, some who are a bit off-center and some who are pretty normal.

"Carrie Fielding will be there. She's coming with her latest disappointment. Freddie Wales. Everybody in town knows he's gay so she gloms onto him and tries to get him to marry her or something. She's bringing him to show the world how broadminded and civilized she is and that she doesn't get hurt when things go wrong in life!

"Everyone knows she's flaky. She'll brood and whine for a week, then find somebody else who isn't going to go for the possessive bit and get her poor heart broken again. She feeds on it. She's masochistic as hell!"

"Yeah. She dated me a few times a couple of weeks ago," John said. "I made it plain from the first that I wasn't about to become a one woman man. She's ... I don't know. It was doomed from the get-go, but she kept trying. I saw her one night at Toro Loco. I was with Freddie – just hitting the spots. No more – and she came in. She said she thought I was going to pick her up and she would go around with me. I told her I would have called if that was the way it was, but tonight I just wanted to play the field a little while. She cornered Freddie and he made the mistake of commiserating about what pigs men were. All of a sudden he found he was going with her. He felt too confined with being with a woman when he wanted a man and broke it off. She told him she was oh so sorry, that she never *meant*...! Which she did, of course.

"She had a big argument with Sarah Levin, claiming she took Dan Downy away from her just to show she could.

"Probably true, knowing Sarah.

"Anyhow, half the people at that club have had run-ins of one kind or another with her."

"She likes being pathetic," Judi said. "She has issues with most of us. I suppose now she'll claim I took you away from her just to be mean.

"George and Bessie Hamilton will be there. You would think they're the most typical married couple in the world, but be alone around him and he's strange to the point of being a pervert. The two of them swing, according to him. He likes to be in bed with two women and another man. He's willing to do anything, wink wink.

"Lonnie Gold is a dream, but he's like you, John. No strings. A good time and move on. He was the first one who broke Sarah's heart when she moved here. No doubt he's broken Carrie's heart, too."

"Talk about perverts, Mike Killian ... well, he'll be there and will be looking for threesomes. It doesn't matter which the other two are," Judi said. "Let's not gossip. It's below us."

"Oh, come on!" Tyna cried. "*Nothing's* below us!"

They soon went out past Crawl Cay to fish, but there wasn't much going on. They went back home refreshed and relaxed. Clint and family stayed home, Judi and John went to the Nine Degrees for dinner and Ben and Earl went into Bocas Town.

In the morning Ben came over to Clint's for some things from the comarca he would use in his plate that night. "It's going to be quite a night, I think. Carrie was in the Barco Hundido with Hank Ford. Hank and Earl are good friends and they weren't on a date. Earl wanted to go to the Pickled Parrot and I didn't. Hank went with him. Carrie went ballistic because her date ran off with some queer. She cooled down and apologized for saying such a thing. She didn't own Hank.

"I told her Earl and Hank were friends. That was all. She said I was a fool to trust him with a man like Hank. I said Hank wasn't gay and didn't do more than have a few drinks with any of them. He'd probably find some tourist surfer chick at the Parrot to spend the night with. Earl would be home. She started on me and I walked out before I told her what I think of a needy masochist who tries to own anyone who's nice to her.

"She'd better can that shit tonight or I'll see that she's the first person ever to be drummed out of the gourmet's club, so help me Jesus!"

"I'm sort of glad we won't be there," Tyna said. "How did she ever get accepted into the club?"

"She's weird and flaky, but she is one *hell* of a cook. I learned a few things from her. I need the achiote because she showed me how to use it."

He soon went home and the Faradays headed for Isla Popa. Tyna's mother's fiftieth birthday.

Clint was older than his wife's mother!

[Ben and Earl came to Charlie's Place with their dishes. They put the plates on the table and noted their numbers, 12, 13 and 14. They talked with Freddie and Hank, who had come as Freddie's guest. John and Judi came in and Judi put their plates on 15 and 16. George and Bessie were 17 and 18. Lonnie Gold came in. Ben had listed him

as his guest. Mike came in with two plates.
George would be his guest.

They mingled and chatted with people. Carrie
was apparently over her bad mood. She was
bubbly and singing. She greeted all the people
who she'd been fighting warmly and said tonight
was going to be special. She could just *feel* it!

Oh, yeah. She was in charge of the festivities
tonight.

About seven she rang the bell for attention and
said it was time to be seated. She would hold up
the snifter with the numbers for singles first. She
drew a number, said, "Nine!" and passed the bowl
above the head of Anne Warner, who drew 17.
Four more drew numbers, then she said the parties
of four. If their number was among those selected,
they could exchange plates with anyone else in
their group. Then three, then two. The group
milled around and found their numbers.

They were all soon seated. They first had the
aperitifs or wine that the club supplied according
to the dish They didn't pay very much attention to
anything but the fine food. It was a gourmet's
delight. These were all very good cooks. They had
to come up with dishes that were served cool or at
room temperature, which was a challenge.

When everyone was finished and drinking the
excellent gourmet coffee blend Carrie stood and

announced, "For dessert, Mona has prepared her famous ... (cough) ... wha...? (cough)." She pitched forward into the table and slid to the floor. Frank Sommers, a medical doctor, was seated three seats away. He ran to her to check her pulse, then her breath, He jerked back from the breath and cried, "My god! She's dead! Cyanide!"]

<u>*A Late Call*</u>

It was nine fifteen when Clint tied the boat to his deck and the family went into the house. The house phone was buzzing. He answered. It was Sergio Sanchez, head of the Bocas del Toro Police Department.

"Clint? Did you know Carrie Fielding?"

"Car ... *did* I know her?"

"She got a big dose of cyanide at some kind of dinner party. It's at Charlie's Place. Ten minutes ago. Can you come over?"

Clint sighed. "I guess so." He told Tyna what had happened. She said she was damned glad they hadn't gone to that one!

Charlie's was only about half a kilometer away. Clint was there in six minutes on his Ho Fai (motorcycle). He went in to find Earl by the door. Earl said Sergio had told him to send Clint right into the dining area. The rest of the guests were mostly on the verandah or in the main salon.

Sergio pointed to the end of the first table where Hank Sommers was kneeling beside Carrie's body. He looked up and nodded, then went back to whatever he was doing. Sergio said that all he knew to that point was that she was making an announcement and keeled over.

Judi was standing to one side. She waved at Clint. He said he would find out what he could from her and a few of the others he knew.

"So. What happened from the time you arrived. Anything out of the ordinary?"

"For this crowd? How could you tell?

"I came in with Hank and put the plates on the table at numbers fifteen and sixteen. We mingled. The talk was general. Fishing, where a special vegetable or cut of meat could be found.

"Carrie was in charge of things tonight. She called us to take our numbers. We would draw a number and take the seats at those numbers. We all drew and took our seats. We had the aperitifs and ate, then had some coffee. Carrie stood and said there was a special dessert, coughed, and dropped.

"Doc Sommers went to her and said she was dead. Cyanide."

"One, the numbers were random, meaning no one could count on her getting the poisoned plate?"

"No one knew who would get what until the drawing."

"So, no one knew where she would be sitting?"

"No ... well, she took the first number and said it

was nine, then we all drew."

"Did anyone go close to her plate from then until you sat to eat?"

"All of us did, I suppose. We were moving around. Nine was at the end of the third table by the wall. John and I drew numbers twenty two and three. We had to walk about two feet away from that seat to get to our table."

"Who was at the same table? Do you know?"

"Freddie Wales, George and Bessie Hamilton and her. Four to a table."

"It's that table where Doc is working on her. Who was at the table to the side?"

"I think Lonnie Gold and Ben and Earl and Anne Warner. Nobody to the front. Hank Ford and Jimmy, Pearl and Gina Smathers were at the only other table you could say was this side on the diagonal."

"Who would want to kill her?"

"Nobody. You avoided her. Sometimes, you felt you would get a kick out of slapping her so hard her teeth would rattle."

"Judi, please give me something! I don't want to have to try to find a nutcase who put cyanide in a plate to see who would get it.

"Who put plate number nine there?"

"I don't know. We could ask." She went into the salon and asked. Sarah Levin.

Sergio had joined them by the time when Judi brought Sarah in. "Okay. You put the dish of basil chicken curry ...." Sergio began.

"No. I brought a pasta dish. Sort of an al fresco thing I make that people like."

"So. Someone just switched plates. It was after she announced her number," Clint said. "Would anyone have noticed?"

"A few will change plates because they get something they know they won't like or that they brought. Nobody's looking. They switch the next plate over," Judi said. "No one will know. They didn't know what they would get until they went to the table."

"Then we're not about to learn who brought the chicken curry," Sergio complained. "You can bet they aren't going to admit it."

"Maybe we can find out!" Judi cried. "I'll get what each person brought when they leave."

"They'll say they brought something else. The food's been eaten and we can't show anything we can prove. The dishes are all covered until just before the drawing," Sergio said.

"Then we have to find who had motive," Clint replied.

"We aren't looking for a random nutcase killer type?" Sergio asked.

"No. Someone deliberately put that plate at

number nine," Judi answered. "I can see that.

"That's a relief, in a way. If it was some nutcase, they would do it again."

"And someone might see how easy it is to get rid of someone when they get pissed," Sergio warned.

"Let's get to her place before anyone here has a chance to beat us to it," Clint suggested. Sergio nodded. He told everyone they could go, unless they saw or heard something that could prove important.

Sergio and Clint went to her house and in, using the keys in her purse. The place was neat enough, but also showed signs of her being a packrat. She had two rooms filled with rows of things. She had a corner of one with a computer desk and a lot of memory sticks and disks and notebooks.

Clint looked at the things in documents when he turned the machine on. It was lists of sites that dealt with antiques and collectibles. The things in those two rooms were all the kinds of things that could become collectibles in a few years or already were to an extent.

There was a document in MSWord that was labeled "To Whom."

That didn't seem like a title anyone would use on a document. To whom it may concern? He double-clicked it. The program loaded and it came onscreen:

I don't know what's going on and am scared. I can't understand why people will treat other people so meanly. I try to live my life as a give and take thing, but I always give and they always take. As soon as I know someone well enough to care about them they always seem to want to use me and discard me.

*What happened is that I had a candy bar I didn't remember buying on the end table by the sofa. I opened it and was about to take a bite and the phone rang and I answered it. I put the candy bar down and went to the kitchen to get a recipe for Anne. When I got back the candy bar was there and the ants had gotten to it. **They were dead!** All those ants were laying around it and they were <u>dead!</u>*

I didn't remember where the candy came from. I didn't remember putting it there. I always eat those Snickers bars right away.

Someone knew I love those things and tried to poison me! I tried to think of who would know my craving for Snickers and think it was someone I was with when I bought one or who saw me when I did. If it had been anything but Snickers I wouldn't even open it.

It would have to be someone who disliked me for some reason. I couldn't think of anyone!

Then I remembered how Sarah Levin and I had

that big argument about Hank Ford. Both of them might do something like that.

That made me remember how Lonnie Gold had tossed me aside and was angered when I saw him at a club and asked why he stood me up. I mean he could have at least called!

Then George or Bessie Hamilton. They wanted me to go to a swinger party and I wouldn't. It angered me no end that they would assume I would ever consider any such thing.

John Marshall. Now he might do something like that. He wanted me to stay away from him and didn't seem to understand that I wanted him away from me as well. He used me shamelessly. Judi Lum is dating him now and might but I don't think she would do anything like that.

Freddie Wales. Would he do anything like that? Is he afraid because I showed him that a woman could care for him more than any man could?

It was poison. That's often a woman's way to kill. Freddie is like a woman that way.

Ben Longstreet or his lover Earl? I sense they don't like the fact men prefer me to them but they aren't really the womanish poisoner type. Ben did beat up those two thugs.

I don't know if I should go to the dinner. All of them will be there and I don't want any scene but I've promised. Maybe it will be alright. I'll put on my happy face and try to avoid them.

*I do want to have the police look into it. I might do that tomorrow morning. That Clint person is a detective and is supposed to come. Maybe he will have some advice. People say he will help anyone and I **do** need help.*

Clint looked up to see Sergio reading over his shoulder. "I think maybe she had named her killer within a few people, don't you?" he asked.

"Oh, yeah. I think, just maybe, she did."

"We know it's not Judi or Ben or Earl. I don't see any of them doing anything like this. Maybe she's right in saying Freddie. He might have been scared, but not because she showed him anything about a woman. Because she would hang on to him whether he liked it or not."

"We'll play holy hell proving anything against anyone suggested by that list," Clint agreed.

"We'll give it the old college try."

"That, we will."

Clint got up early in the morning and headed for the Golden Grill to see what the latest gossip was about. That it would be about Carrie Fielding was foregone.

Jim said she was a rather strange type of person. Needy and clinging. People didn't like that. Bill said he had almost gotten trapped by her, but saw what she was and stayed away. Tom (who Clint did _not_ like) said she had chased him shamelessly ever since she came to the island and he had a hard time staying where she couldn't get to him.

That could be discarded. If there was anyone in Bocas Town she wouldn't be attracted to, it was him. He had moved to Ecuador and was back in less than two months. It seemed he was better than anybody there and was out of "his element."

He was out of his element anywhere.

Arny said he had spoken with her, but she didn't seem to have any interest in him. She went for the macho bodybuilder types, which no one at that table except maybe Clint fit. She didn't go after married men, so Clint was out.

"She went after that queer, Freddie!" Tom spat.

"And he's in a lot better shape than most of us," Arny replied. "He's active. I keep threatening to get into shape, but I'm too lazy. Besides, Mary likes me the way I am. I'm not looking and I'm not doing without."

"I think her killer is very clever," Jim said. "The way it was done will probably make it hard to impossible to catch her killer, won't it, Clint?"

"Yeah. It won't be too hard to find out who, but it'll be hell to prove."

"So all but the one who did it will want you to find out and prove it. There will be suspicion enough to go around and it will stick if you can't prove different.

"Clever, and a woman's method. That would fit Freddie, Sarah and Bessie. Of them, I'd opt for Bessie. She can be scheming and she has tried a bit of blackmail. It didn't work, but that's in her."

"You?" Tom asked, perking up.

"No. A friend who was at a party she was attending. He didn't want her and she resented it. She tried to blackmail him with some photos she would show his business partner and his parents."

"What did he do?" Tom asked.

"He told her he takes a few pictures himself. He had the perfect one to laminate on her tombstone. It seems she decided not to try that on him again. He's the type who might actually cut her throat for her.”

Tom started on a story about someone who tried to blackmail him because he went out with Maria Pendleton and didn’t know that she was married and how he handled it. Clint stood up and nodded at the others.

“Going?” Jim asked, with a smirk. He knew how Tom made Clint ready to smack him in the puss.

“Yeah. That reminded me. I’d forgotten I had to meet with Maria Pendleton about that lot she has for sale next to mine. I might want to buy it to get a bigger lawn. I’ll chide her about running around with Tom and not telling him she was married.”

“Oh! I didn’t mean ... I mean, we didn’t ... it was all innocent! It was about some land she was listing!” Tom cried.

Jim was now giggling so hard there were tears running down his face. “You’ll never learn, will you?” he asked. Tom looked blank. Arny was giggling.

Clint always wondered why that ass was always there. The others put up with his never-ending stream of bullshit. No matter what anyone knew or had done, he could beat it. Clint was surprised when he didn’t start a silly story about the time he was murdered.

He had to agree with one thing. The killer was being clever. This one tried to leave it where there would never be anything but suspicion on all of them. There would never be enough proof of anything to convict a single one. There would be reasonable doubt no matter what.

He went on to the station. Sergio had all her memory sticks and disks there. He said she read a lot. Dave would get a kick out of the fact she had downloaded all of his Nick Storie books

"Clint, there's nothing here that would clear anyone and nothing that would convict anyone."

"I know, Sergio. We're dealing with a very sick personality in her. She spent her time around a few other sick people and a few more who would bolster her inferiority complex. I want to trace what I can of her past history. I want to know if there's anyone from her past here."

He nodded and looked thoughtful. "Maybe she screwed up some people's lives before she came here and they found her?"

"That's a distinct possibility. She probably left quite a trail of people she screwed up, one way or another. It probably wasn't intentional – I should say *consciously* intentional – but it was there. It's part of her personality."

"Well, you've got your own method with the computer. Maybe you can find something. I'll go out to her house and see if I can find anything more in that mess. I think she would be the type to keep a diary. I'll find that if I can. It should at least give us hints."

Clint had to agree that finding a diary might well give them some insight, but it would be damned dull reading.

He went to the internet and to her name with a Google search, then with a Yahoo! search. Very little. She was born in Kensington, Kentucky. The family moved to Rochester, New York, when she was three years old. They had moved to Madison, Wisconsin, when she was five. She had gone to grammar school there. She was a shy student. Her mother died when she was twelve of lung cancer. She had withdrawn and wouldn't show emotion from that time. Her father raised her as best he could, until he remarried when she was fourteen. They soon moved to Bakersfield, California. She finished schooling there. She was shy and didn't have many friends. It was noted she seemed disoriented anytime she was away from her father for more than a few days. He was once investigated for child abuse, but was cleared absolutely. The symptoms she exhibited were from feeling abandoned by everyone except him since the death of her mother . He died in an industrial accident at a petrochemical plant where he was employed when she was sixteen. She lived with her stepmother until she was graduated from high school as an above average student, then dropped out of sight. She was twenty seven when she died.

That surprised Clint. He thought she was in her mid thirties.

There was simply nothing anywhere about those eleven years since she left Bakersfield.

He sat back to think and shook his head. Sergio called to say he'd found the diaries. There were fourteen of them. She had the first one she started when her mother died until today.

Clint went to the house. She had a very neat handwriting and wrote mostly very short notes. "Today we went to Disneyworld. Big deal!"

"Daddy got a raise today. He's the best worker they have."

"I went to the market to do the shopping today. Daddy says I did real good. Better than even my Mom had done and she was good!"

"Daddy says I'm as good a cook as Mom was. She was the world's best."

Next year: "I feel sorry for Daddy. He doesn't have anyone but me to come home to and I know how men need a woman. I told him he has to get another wife or a woman to come home to and that's how I feel and there! He said he would always have Mom to compare and no other woman could ever replace her. I said that it wasn't a matter of replacing anybody. It was a matter of not letting his life come to a stop. He said he had me and I said that was true and always would be but we are talking about reality not what we want it to be. He must not allow himself to become a robot that just keeps going to no purpose. No argument. Find a woman. He is human and he has needs."

"Daddy met Virginia and likes her because she reminds him of Mom. I told him to be careful. Mom is gone. Don't try to bring her back. It's impossible."

"Daddy met Martha and really likes her. He confided it was mostly sex but she is a good woman and she understands him. She had a bad marriage and nasty divorce. They will get along because they both have a big painful past."

Next year: "Martha and I get along better than I thought would be possible. She is going to marry Dad. I think she will make him happy again. I pray to a god I don't believe in that he will be happy."

"Dad and Martha went to San Francisco for their honeymoon. Dad wanted me along but I said that would be the stupidest thing he ever did. It was their honeymoon and it was the only one they would have and they didn't need some brat along. Have fun and forget I exist. He said he loves me so much it hurts. It's like Mom was telling him it was alright to go on living."

"Dad has a new job or a promotion at least. He will work in the field again which is what he likes. It's dangerous sometimes but he likes that."

"I have to find ways to occupy my time. I have tried dating and I tried the sex thing but it didn't make me feel much of anything. Danny the man I was with is very nice and I do like him. If he wants sex I don't care. I'll try to make it good for him."

Next year: "I think I can use this sex thing but I'm also afraid it is using me. I don't understand why I have to be with some guy who only wants to be with me because I'm an easy piece of ass for him. I'm neutral about the sex but I have to be with him. I'm fucked up in my head I guess. I want to be with him and to touch him and sleep with him but I don't want the sex. You can't have one without the other."

"I don't get myself sometimes. I don't care if I'm with Frank much but I get all jealous if he even talks to another girl. I don't really want him but I don't want anyone else to have him. I need a shrink!"

"Oh my God! I've been crying for two days! I can't stop! Dad is dead! A big tank fell and crushed him! I don't want to live! Oh God take me now!"

There was a blank to the end of the year and for a month of the next, then: "I'm past the worst part. I can go on but I don't care. I met Gordon today and he lost his mother and father at the same time when the bus they were in went over the cliff in Oregon. We sort of mesh. He's the first one since Dad died I've slept with and it was sort of nice and warm. I don't think we either one wanted sex but we needed it. It woke me up. I'll write more now that I'm reasonably sane. I do need a man in my life. I can't feel safe without one. I just hope there are no more of those users who don't understand about people."

"Gordy just walked out! He said it's been great but he has to get on. He's turning into a vegetable here. It sort of hurt but I understand. I want to get away from this place. I'm stagnating."

Next year: "I was in Bogota for forty eight hours. I like it. I like the Latin culture."

"I was used again. Willie Wonka as I call him got what he wanted and went straight to a cheap whore on the street when he left. He says he was only talking to her and bought her a drink but I'm not that stupid. He said he'd better find someone who understands him. I wished him luck."

"That Donna bitch just as much as drug Stan away from me in the bar! What's wrong with me?

I get to where I like a guy then some cheap slut just prances in and takes him! Men are so <u>stupid</u>! I wish I could be like that. Use him and walk away. I get to where I need him and he goes anyway. What's <u>wrong</u> with me!?"

"Great gods of yore! I got gonorrhea somewhere from one of those asshole men! I caught it and it's cured but this is a warning to myself to be careful. There are worse things than the claps out there."

"I'm moving to Nicaragua or somewhere. If I stay here I'll end up slitting my wrists. You can't ever trust a man. They're all the same. As soon as they see you might want them they disappear. Most other women want to take him just to show they can. Wiggle their ass and he drools all over the floor. Men are animals and women are bitches."

There were a lot of descriptions. She certainly had enough lovers that she should have caught on that they would be gone as soon as she started clinging and making demands.

There were such notes about all their suspects. They had all, in her mind, used her and discarded her. The women were in competition to see if they could take away her men as soon as she got them. She was seriously thinking of moving to Bogota. She had really liked it there.

Clint shook his head and sat back. "Anything get

cleared up?" Sergio asked.

"Other than that she was a serious neurotic most of her life, no."

"Anyone here mentioned?"

"All of them and more. A few notes on how wonderful they were, then suspicion, then she got dumped for no reason except that men are pigs and women are bitches who only want to take her men away to prove that they can. She kept asking what was wrong with her. She never saw what was so plain to everyone else."

"So the suspects remain."

"Nothing's changed there!"

Clint sighed and went home to his wife, who was having a great time with a roomful of people from the church who wanted to teach her how to raise children the way God decreed. It seemed some people who were there to see if they should establish a missionary project in Bocas del Toro had met her little baby boy in the streets. They been shocked that he was so knowledgeable about the horrors and evils of sex. She should be teaching him that Satan had representatives everywhere who would surely lead him into the evil horrors of perversion.

"Really?" Clint asked, innocently. "Why would God make sex so compelling it would destroy a person, then make rules against doing anything with it?"

"Satan lead us into depravity!" one of them intoned.

"Bullshit!" Nito replied. "If God didn't want us to have sex, why didn't he make it feel different? Why make it feel so good?

"I can't wait until I'm old enough to see what it's like. Everybody I know who is old enough spends all their time talking about it."

"That is God's fight with Satan! He wants us to live clean decent lives!"

"But God is the only one who can create. Why would he create us to where Satan can do anything? That's just plain silly."

"We're here to explain these things," one said, piously. "We're representatives of the true way."

"God can create us and the universe and all that, but he needs you to tell us about it? He can create a universe, but can't tell the people he creates what he wants himself?"

"We have free will. We must each chose our own path!" she said, stiffly.

"So I choose the path where I like sex. Mom, can I go to the parque? That funny old man who keeps trying to feel me up wants to buy me some helados."

Talk about shocked looks! One of them actually fainted. Nito said that was quite a bit of an overreaction, wasn't it?

"Be back before dark, Honey. I do worry if you're out too late. You're so cute some gringa might want to molest you, and you know it's alright, if it's a woman, but I'm not sure that's right myself. That's gringo thinking."

Nito went out. Clint looked amused. Tyna was about to explode in laughter.

"He's putting you on about the pervert," Clint said. "I think he just wants you to see yourselves as we see you. A comedy act.

"Tyna, this murder is damned weird. I think I know what happened and why, but there's no way I can get a handle on it. I don't want this one to get away with it. Too many people will be affected."

"Murder? Do you mean that poor defenseless woman who was poisoned at that wild party?" a woman asked. "What do you have to do with it?"

"It was a dinner party. There was nothing wild about it. She was not a poor defenseless woman. I'm a detective and am investigating it."

"But I heard it was almost an orgy and that the most depraved people in Bocas Town were there! A man who everybody knows and respects here told me about it. He was passing just after they found her body and helped the police at first, but he isn't an official investigator. They couldn't allow him to continue."

"Tom?"

"Yes, that was his name, I believe."

"He's a joke and was nowhere near the scene. The police would laugh him out of the place if he was. They didn't find her body. She died right in front of thirty four people. A couple are what we would call depraved, but almost all of the people there were decent upstanding citizens. Tom is known by everyone here as the island's top bullshit artist. No one respects him."

"But there were homosexuals and other perverts there! I've met Freddie Wales. I tried to counsel him about his evil ways, but he wouldn't hear me!"

"Freddies' no pervert. He's a little swishy, but he's a good person," Tyna said. "Ben and Earl were there. They're gay. We're close friends. We go fishing together a lot. They're also very good decent people.

"I don't know if there were other gay people there. Most in the area are bisexual. Nobody here cares.

"Clint, I have to go after Nicole. She's at Ben's with Judi. I suppose they're getting tired of taking care of her, but I had to get that stuff from the docks. She didn't want to go along."

"Nicole is your baby daughter? You let her go to

those *homosexuals*' house?"

"Yes. They're gay, not pedophiles," Clint said. "Get off your holier-than-thou horse here or these people will run you off the island fast. We won't interfere with your lives so long as you don't interfere with ours.

"Tyna, I'm going to be tied up with this murder awhile, I guess. I'll have to interview a lot of people. Maybe someone can either confirm or deflate my ideas."

"You have a candidate for the killer?"

"Uh-huh. It's based on personalities and on a case or two I had when I first came here. I'll have to talk with Doc Sommers."

"She had a STD?" Tyna asked.

"She had gonorrhea in the past. It's more than possible. If she spread something nasty to some-one, they may want revenge or something."

"If they don't fornicate, they don't have to worry about such things!" a woman declared, haughtily.

"Get a grip! Weren't you leaving?" Tyna asked.

They stood and filed out. Tyna laughed. Clint shook his head and sighed. The whole world was weird lately.

He went to the station. He was at a loss as to what to look at next. He was sure he had it figured fairly close, but how could he prove a word of it?

Clint studied the diaries a bit more, particularly since she moved to Bocas Town. They weren't very easy to read. The handwriting was excellent, but the subject and slant was confusing and dull. She blamed everyone around her for the things she brought on herself. The tale was disturbing. Clint wondered if she was blackmailing someone. It would fit the personality type, though there was no hint of that in the diaries.

Clint could figure what would happen with a lot of people. He was able to follow the way they thought. An insecure person would act in a certain way, but this was a lot more than simple insecurity. It was also a bit more than paranoia. It was more than inferiority complex. It was more than displacement.

Her mental path was confusing even to her. The diaries said that plainly. "What is <u>wrong</u> with me?" was written too many times. It was usually after something that showed what was wrong with her in unequivocal terms. She would not see it. *None is so blind...* Clint thought.

He would have to try to follow her mental path

maps. That was going to be a pretty heavy task. It looked too much like the paths branched at odd times in odd directions. She was totally rational most of the time, then was off on an unexpected tangent. She hadn't shown her actual thought patterns in everyday life. People considered her odd, but not as weird as she was.

Clint was sure he had this one figured. He had to know if she was, indeed, blackmailing anyone. He had to know if she had pushed someone too far with her clinging. He had to know if she had taken some odd kind of revenge on another woman. He had to know what really went on with Freddie.

Maybe that was a place to start down this weird and disjointed mental path. He went to the station and asked Sergio where he could find Freddie, if he knew.

"He's staying with Eduardo Pinz. Out behind the airport."

He went to the place. Freddie was laying in a hammock on the front porch. He said he had a hell of a hangover.

"I have to know what happened between you and Carrie. It could be important."

"I didn't kill her. It wasn't that kind of thing. I couldn't, anyhow.

"I knew her off and on since she moved here. She wasn't interested in me until one night in

Toro Loco when some guy left her there. She said she thought they had a standing date and he said they didn't. She was whining about it and I made the mistake of sympathizing with her. She was all of a sudden dating me! It never happened!

"I couldn't get away from her easy. I had to tell her I'm gay and never asked to date her. I slept with her once because we got a little drunk and I went home with her. I didn't expect that and didn't much care for it.

"She said I was just scared because I was afraid she'd change me. It was pure horse shit!

"Anyhow, she apologized the next day and said it was a misunderstanding and I had just used her to see if I would like a woman. She didn't mind. I very obviously didn't. We could still be friends, even though it would be hard for her because she really did like me.

"It was purely awful! I tried to avoid her. I did, mostly."

"Did she tell you anything about anyone else specific?"

"She told me about everyone specific! Everyone on the island and in the world just used and abused her, then, what she said, 'Discarded' her. Her deepest hurt was Lonnie. I can see why. He's a walking dream. The one she never did anything with and who she secretly wanted more than anyone was Earl, but he was Ben's. That was set in steel. He would never relate to a woman.

"I can see him as a walking dream and he's always nice to me, but she's right in saying he and Ben are it. They'll stay together for life, I'd bet. I can picture him as a stud, but he doesn't do women."

"He's bi. He was going with a woman when he met Ben. They just took one look at each other and he decided he would be much better off and happier with Ben than with a woman. Ben also has a lot of experience with women. They just fit together I guess."

"If their women were anything like Carrie I can see why they don't want women anymore!"

Clint laughed. "Did she say anything much about women?"

"Well, yes. She definitely thought she was in competition with any woman who came around. She thought all of them were pretending to be friends, but women are always competitive and only pretend to be friends to impress men, who really can be friends with other men so they don't understand that women can't be friends.

"She was a weird fucked-up mess."

"That's the consensus. Any specific women she disliked especially?"

"Well, Bessie Hamilton the most. She hated

Sarah Levin with a passion. She said that's why she was extra sweet toward them. Watch who a woman is overly-nice to and you'll know she despises her.

"She was confused about Judi. She said Judi sometimes seemed to actually be able to have women friends. Maybe because she was Oriental. They're like a different species. She said most women are on the order of morons and idiots, but Judi is intelligent. That makes her scary."

"She was really a weird person. Thanks."

Freddie waved and Clint left. The diaries hinted at such thoughts.

Carrie Fielding had been crazier than the proverbial loon!

Clint went back to the station to check with the computer on Carrie's father and stepmother.

Father was as already seen. Her stepmother was Alice Andover nee Alice Danforth, Pittsburgh, Pennsylvania. She had a normal life through her teens and had married Gerald Andover, had a daughter with him, Judith. There was a nasty divorce where Andover was able to show she was an unfit mother in a way that seemed contrived. She was bitter about it and fought for years to get her daughter back. She met Fielding and married him. She was able to transfer her love for her biological daughter to Carrie. The time with her was good for her, for Fielding and for Carrie.

Since Fielding's death she had resided near Bakersfield, running a little restaurant that was popular. She had sold the restaurant a year ago and had retired. She was now living in Managua, Nicaragua (!) with her biological daughter and the daughter's husband and two children. She had one of the happy endings to the removal of the daughter from her life. She had been reunited with the daughter four years ago. They had become close.

So! Did Carrie know that the daughter was back in her stepmother's life? Did she then feel the daughter had stolen her stepmother away? It would fit the way she thought.

Clint got the diaries from the time four years ago when the daughter/ mother reunion happened. There was a mention the first time:

"Mom Alice met her daughter for the first time since the divorce. She said it was a little formal but she immediately felt a mother's love. Maybe they will meet again. It may be good for them both. I know better than anyone what it was like to be separated from my mother and how I wanted nothing more than to be with her just one more time."

"Mom Alice and her daughter Judith have been seeing each other every Saturday. Judith is married to a man from Nicaragua who owns a restaurant. I was even there once! She may move to Managua next year. Her husband has to be closer to the place or they will steal him blind."

"Mom is going to move down to Nicaragua with Judith! Maybe that will be good for them both, but what about me? That's stupid! I left her in Bakersfield. Why would she be abandoning me? I abandoned her! I'm really fucked up! Why do I get this way? Am I crazy? What's wrong with me?"

There was no more mention of Mom Alice. Did she simply erase her from her life?

Clint went back to the earlier diaries. He was going to follow another path with this.

He spent some hours making a list of people she had dated or known well enough to mention. Not one of them was mentioned in any way after they had their breakup of whatever type breakup they had. Only her mother for awhile after her death, and her father for even longer after his death.

Was he right? Did she simply erase them from her life at that point? Was that why she didn't get the connection that showed they would dump her when she got clingy and possessive?

She had asked that one time if she was crazy. Never before, never again.

"Yeah, Carrie. You were crazy as a loon. You

hid it very well!”

There was little more to be learned from the diaries. Clint looked at the clock and did a jerky double-take. It was after midnight! He called Tyna, who said she figured he would be gone and forget what time it was when he left. He was in that displaced mood where he seemed to be somewhere else in his mind.

“We have to do something about Nito. That preacher, Dawson, came with one of the women, the one who thinks she’s their spokesman. Nicole let them in before I knew who was there.

“Anyhow, Nito was swimming and came in without a stitch on. The silly woman said it was disgraceful for me to let him run around the house nude. He asked her why. He said, so far as he knew, he had the same parts in the same places in the same general size and shape as all the other boys, so what’s the big deal?

“She started on about perverts seeing him. He said the only perverts who would be in the house are friends and that they’d know you would kill them slow and painful if they tried anything with him. She was just scared of sex and didn’t want anybody else to have it.

“Clint, I know he’s smarter than most of the gringo and black and Latina kids here, but he deliberately baits those kind of people. Someday he's going to get in trouble with it or get us in trouble.

"Dawson was looking at him like ... if you ask me there *was* a pervert in the room.

"I told them I wasn't interested in hearing about how they raised their kids to be afraid of life. If they looked around they could see that the Indio kids were happy and secure and balanced. They couldn't show me that in any of their kids. I asked them to leave.

"Dawson just sat there. I think he had a hard-on and didn't dare to stand. He said he just wanted one more word, a quote from the scriptures, and for Nito to put on some clothes, then he'd go.

"You could see he was trying to think of a scripture to quote so he said, 'Leviticus eighteen twenty two states clearly that homosexuality is an abomination to God. You take the chance of sending your soul straight to hell!'

"I didn't see any connection. Nito said so was eating crustaceans or shellfish. Leviticus something or other. Did he like to eat lobster?

"I wonder where he got that? It's apparently true. Dawson got up with his briefcase in front of his crotch. He was beet-red in the face. He said something about pagan Indios. Nito said he'd tell all his friends what he said. Maybe he wouldn't see any of them in his stupid church.

"Clint! He's only four going on five! I would expect something like that from an Indio boy twelve or thirteen or from the others at eighteen or twenty, not five!"

"He likes to investigate things. He's better on the comp than I am. He can read on a colegio level, what we'd call high school in the states. He has a very logical mind. When things don't make sense he sees it.

"I'll be home soon. I think I've learned something I always suspected."

"What's that?"

"Carrie Fielding was as crazy as a loon!"

"Oh. I knew that. Come on home. We can try some of that sex stuff Nito talks about."

He laughed and said he'd be right there!

Clint stretched and laid back in the hammock. Nito was laying on him. He had a cup of coffee and Nito had a glass of banana/pineapple chicha. Nito snuggled against him and said, "I love you, Dad. I want to go to the comarca and not come here again for fifty years. These people are a pain in the ass. They think everything you do is wrong or evil or something."

"A thing is evil if you think it's evil when you do it. If it's something natural, it isn't evil. It's evil if you try to make someone do something they don't want to do, but you know that because you've been raised to not ask people to do the things they don't want to do.

"I take it this is about that preacher yesterday?"

"You said a pervert would do things and act in weird ways. He kept staring at my pinga like he never saw one before."

"So Tyna said. You didn't perchance have to scratch or something just about then?"

He laughed and said he might have had to rub or something right about then.

"Don't bait those people, son. I'm serious. They

can lose control. Okay?"

"Okay, Dad. I sort of thought it was stupid to do that. Later." He snuggled closer.

What would they say if they saw us right now? Both of us nude and actually touching?

They finished their beverages after a few more minutes and went swimming. Judi came onto her deck and waved. She usually wagged a finger at Clint when he was nude out on the deck in the morning. It was a sort of set ritual since he had moved there.

They swam for about fifteen minutes, then climbed out to rinse in the shower on the deck.

When they had dried and put on some clothes Tyna asked what Clint was going to be doing this morning.

"Eliminations. I'm going to have to do this the Sherlock Holmes way, I suppose."

He played with Nicole and Nito for awhile, then said he'd better get at it.

"Clint, should I start getting our things together for Cusapín?"

He nodded. He was getting sick of Bocas Town and people trying to run their lives. It would be good to get back where he felt he belonged.

He went to the station. He didn't really know what his next step would be. He thought about Carrie's way of thinking on his way. He was sure he could find something at her house so he and Sergio went there.

"Where and what?" Sergio asked.

"I don't know – and I don't know. She kept everything on her computer. Maybe something's there. We haven't gone through a lot of those memory sticks."

"I've been thinking about that blackmail angle. If she has something on that line it'll be on those things. It's just one hell of a lot to have to go through."

"C'est la vie."

He sat and booted the computer. He checked everything on it, then took the first of the twenty some-odd memory sticks to insert into the USB port. There was nothing that caught his eye. It was mostly data concerning the collectibles.

The second was much the same.

The third had some correspondence on it. He read it. Mostly forums and so forth to do with the collectibles.

The fourth was about Central America. Maps and information for tourists. It wasn't completely filled. There was a little about a court case in California having to do with child custody. It was from nine years ago?

Nothing else.

Fifth was pictures taken around the Americas. It

was full. He scanned quickly through. A first section was Mexico, then Nicaragua, then Costa Rica, then Colombia, then back to Panamá. Almost half the 4 gig stick was Panamá.

Sixth was Dave's Nick Storie novels with a couple of CD Grimes and three of the newer ones. *Inverted Paradise, Good Bi,* and *View From the Middle,* all about people discovering their bisexuality. There were several other books by known authors. Lawyer/courtroom dramas.

Was she discovering that she was bisexual or a lesbian?

Clint didn't think that would be it. She wasn't either. She was closer to asexual.

Seventh was a jumble. It had a lot of short notes about any number of subjects.

Clint remembered Dr. Sommers. He asked Sergio if he had learned if she had any STDs or such. No.

What was that part about evidence gathering and proof? Why had she been studying that?

Lots of notes about local things. She had twice started to write a book. Clint looked at the first few paragraphs and decided she didn't have the talent to write.

He got to the end. Nothing.

He put the eighth stick into the port and noticed the box by the individual file:

PEZ: modified 9/16/10
4KB

He sat back, thought, then put the seventh stick in the second port. He put the arrow on a file:

mybk: modified 6/29/11
12.7KB

A book. Last year. Maybe he would find how her mind was working then. He could read a few pages. Maybe he would find something.

Angeline went into the bath to refresh before going to the party. She would be certain to make a splash with her new D'Or outfit and Guchi purse and shoes. That stupid Wandalee bitch would have some competition for a change. She certainly deserved it.

Her eyes. She needed a bit more blue shadow. The false lashes bothered her a little, but she could live with that.

It was going to be a real blast! She was at last going to show that bunch of two-bit whores who was best at the game. Forty people who hated her were going to hate her even more when tonight was over! Forty cheap sluts and forty pigs, like all men were.

Well good! Tonight she was going to have her choice. She'd get the one most wanted and dump him like Rodney had dumped her!

She adjusted her bra a little and swept regally

out and to the stairs, where she was making her grand entrance. She was smiling brightly at the gathering and moving slowly down the stairs with her hips swinging provocatively.

Eat your hearts out, bitches!

She stepped from the bottom step and offered her hand to Arthur, the second most piggy pig there. She could tell by his eyes how he wanted her.

One chance was all you got bastard!

A voice behind her called, "Angeline!" and she turned with a bright smile on her face.

Then, blackness.

Lt. Eviline Marston shook her head and sighed. She hated this! A murder with an untraceable poison with eighty suspects. There would never be enough evidence against any of them to convict. That meant seventy nine who would spend the rest of their lives under suspicion.

"Frank! Front and center!" she ordered.

It went on for a couple more pages like that. It was a formula trash novel that had no style and a weak plot backed by unbelievable characters. She had written that first few pages and apparently knew it was garbage.

Next was another attempt:

mybk2: modified 3/14/12

9.4KB

Nancy knew it was stupid to think this way. She was only going to sink deeper into a morass of a sick world where she knew she didn't belong.

She knew at that moment that she was not going to continue living a life in this black hell that others made for her. It wasn't worth it. Her mind was made up. All she wanted was for those who had put her through this miserable hell to pay.

And pay they would!

She had to select the right time. She knew Tuesday was the slowest day for going anywhere or doing anything in Fairest Dell Village. It was a night everyone would be home watching TV or chatting on their computers. It was perfect!

So! It would be Tuesday!

It would have to be fast. She didn't relish a painful death at all.

She had it!

Capt. Florence Gilders looked at the scene and shook her head sadly. A woman murdered in cold blood in the middle of a peaceful little village. She was disliked by many there and not one of them would have a decent alibi, except for the nine married couples who would have been together. Of course, two could have conspired to kill her. A wife and her husband.

It was a very clever setup. A rope with a heavy

lead ball hooked to a tree branch over the footpath Nancy would be using. A trip wire. She tripped the wire and the ball had swung down to crush the side of her head. At least she didn't suffer.

There wouldn't be any way she could solve this one unless someone saw something. More than fifty people were going to spend the rest of their lives under suspicion of murder.

"Edwards! Front and center!" she yelled.

It went on for a bit in that vein. Clint had his answer. It was what he had suspected from the first.

He sighed and stood. Sergio asked if he found any leads in that stuff.

"Yeah. It's what I thought from the first."

"Who do I arrest?"

"No one. The killer's dead."

"Dead? No one's dead, except Carrie Fielding!"

"Yep! Let's go back to the station and I'll write it up."

They headed back. Sergio was thinking all the way. Just as they reached the station he made a sound, then asked, "Announcing her number. She wouldn't take the first one. She'd take the last!

"Okay. The way you figure it is that she palmed number nine and switched her poisoned plate to there when she passed close to the table. People were avoiding her and wouldn't have noticed. Nine was close to where every one of them would pass when they drew their number. She set it up to get even with them all? Did those book things tell you that?"

"Yeah. The first one was a murder that they wouldn't be able to solve because everyone in the room hated the victim. The fact that it would be easy to solve wasn't seen by her. Only two or three were close enough to the victim to have done it. She noticed that and stopped.

"The second was written last month. A setup where it was a suicide made to look like a murder where everyone in town would be suspects. She overlooked the fact that it wasn't a situation the suicide could manage on her own.

"She missed the details we look for in a murder case. If she'd simply held the number 'til last it would have a better chance."

"She wouldn't be able to announce the number when others would still have time to make the switch."

"A detail. She missed it."

"It's enough for me. Do you think it'll clear it up enough that there won't still be a lot of suspicion? After all, we haven't proven anything. It's conjecture."

"I think we can prove it. We know what the

killer recipe was. She made the stuff that afternoon, meaning the ingredients will be in her kitchen. If she dumped them, it will still tell us. Every one of them is used in other recipes. It's a matter of the combination."

Sergio nodded and they went back to the house and to the kitchen. Clint went through the recipes and noted that she was, like most truly good cooks, not using exact measurements. He found the recipe for the killer meal in the very back of the file. All the spice and condiment ingredients were on the front of the shelf in almost the order the recipe called for. There were three kinds of cheese, all of which were in the refrigerator and all of which had some used. The pasta box was in the trash can along with the chicken bones.

"I think that will tie it up tight. Shall we go file a report for the record?" Sergio said. Clint agreed. They went to the station and added it all up. It was plenty solid. No one here would be looking for silly technicalities to have anything thrown out.

Then Clint went home.

"That's about everything," Tyna said. "We can leave most of it here. Judi can take care of it. We have a boatload now! It's a good thing ninety percent of the clothes can stay."

"I'll lock up and we can give Judi the keys on the way out. Where are Nito and Nicole?"

"They went to say goodbye to their friends. They'll be back in a few minutes. Nito wants to get away from here. So does Nicole.

"Oh, for pity's sake! Give me a damned break!"

Nito, Nicole and Preacher Dawson and Mildred Samms, the church woman, were coming along the sidewalk.

Clint snorted and went to the front door. Nito came in with Nicole. He blocked the door to the preacher and Samms.

"We were merely making certain the children got back home safely," Samms said, accusingly. Dawson sniffed.

"They have five hundred times before. Why wouldn't they now?"

"They are mere children! They shouldn't be wandering the streets, alone!"

"They have a few hundred friends between here and town. They aren't alone. Ever. That's what you don't get about the Indio culture.

"Dawson, do you understand the law and what we do about pedophiles here?"

"I imagine there are some laws here. There are everywhere. They are not always enforced."

"You should know what it is, in reality. You'd understand why there's only very rarely any kind of problem here."

"Surely that wasn't serious!" Samms cried. "The child said he would yell and that horrible policeman would *shoot* anyone who bothered him!"

"And what did Sergio say to that?"

"Er, that he would shoot anyone who tried to force a child to ... do anything."

"*Shoot* them?!" Dawson yelled.

"Yes. This woman being with you today may have saved your life, huh?

"We're going to the comarca. We won't be back for some time. I don't like for my children to be around people who've been taught to worry about such things. They too often are the problem, not the solution.

"Adios!"

He closed the door in their faces and went to the deck. The kids got in the boat and they headed for

Cusapín.

"I think it's time for a time out!" Clint declared.

"You deserve one!" Tyna replied.

"We all deserve a time out of Bocas," Nito said. "What a bunch of ridiculous clowns! I wonder what world they're from."

"Not one I want to live in," Tyna said. "I'm getting like Nito. I don't care if I don't see Bocas for the next fifty years or so."

"There isn't anything to do here," Nito said. "I mean, those kids my age don't do anything but play and look for trouble. Even Samuél was looking for a way to steal some candy bars at the China. He wanted me to do something to make the girl look away from the TV. I told him I wasn't a thief and went out. I didn't even say adios to him. I didn't know he would do that. He never did before."

"Don't let your life go down that path," Clint warned. "With this case I've learned what going down the wrong path can do to you. It's not something to take any pride in."

"That preacher said he'd buy me a candy bar," Nicole said. "I told him candy rots your teeth."

"If he or anyone else tries to put his hands on you you are to yell for Sergio, there, or for anyone nearby, on the comarca," Tyna instructed.

"I was right by the door and he saw I was

watching him. He said something about that being true and went away. That stupid old biddie saw him and they said they would walk back with us. I said we knew the way, but they came anyway," Nito said.

"I told Judi about that one. She says she already has Sergio watching him. I think he should be sent back where he came from."

"If we're lucky, I mean Panamanians, Sergio will, shall we say, encourage him to look for a church elsewhere. Elsewhere being anywhere but Panamá."

They chatted about all kinds of things for the two hours to Cusapín. It was damned good to be home!

C. D. Moulton's works are available on most major outlets as printed or e-books. CD writes the CD Grimes, PI, mysteries, the Det. Lt. Nick Storie mysteries, the Clint Faraday mysteries, the Flight of the Maita science fiction series, books on orchid culture and many others of many types. Mystery, adventure, intrigue, science fiction, humor, fantasy, paranormal, mild erotica, and factual.